If Flowers Could Talk

written by Brigette Harrington

illustrated by Tatiana Rusakova

ABEO BOOKS

If Flowers Could Talk

Copyright © 2021 by Brigette Harrington
Illustrated by Tatiana Rusakova
ABEO BOOKS, Hillsboro, Oregon

For more information go to: www.AbeoBooks.com

Dedication

This book is dedicated to my two amazing grandmothers,
affectionately known as "Amma" Shirlene and "Nana" Charline.
Thank you for your love and for being so special to me. You have both
always helped me notice the smallest of details, and you help me find
beauty in everyday life. I am one lucky girl
to have such loving grandmothers.

JOIN ME AS I JOURNEY AND FLY THROUGH MY GARDENS,
A BLISSFUL SIGHT TO BEHOLD.
MY FLOWERS, THEY TALK AND THEY SHARE AND THEY DAZZLE,
LISTEN TO THEIR STORIES UNFOLD.

LOOK CLOSELY MY FRIENDS, FOR INDEED YOU WILL SEE,
HIDDEN ON EACH PAGE IS A LITTLE BUMBLE BEE.
NESTLED AMONG FLOWERS, LEAVES, AND THE TREES,
HE IS ALWAYS THERE WAITING, LOOKING FOR YOU AND ME.

BEFORE I BLOOM I'M CURLED UP TIGHT,
HIDING MY BODY— A BEACON OF LIGHT.
OUT I POP, SHAPED LIKE A CONE,
A HEDGEHOG TOP, A WINGED CREATURES' DREAM THRONE.

I am a Coneflower

MY FLOWER'S MOUTH LOOKS JUST LIKE A TOAD
AND MY LEAVES RESEMBLE A FLAX.
MIGHTY AND STRONG, I SPREAD MY ROOTS AMONG,
SPEWING SEEDS ALONG ALL OF MY TRACKS.

I'm a Toadflax

LOOK AT ME WITH MY BELLS SO BLUE,
RINGING, CHIMING, CALLING TO YOU.
MY NECK IS HEAVY WITH FRILLY BLOSSOMS OF LACE,
THAT SMELL SO GOOD WHEN YOU SNIFF MY SWEET FACE.

I'm a Bluebell

NATURE IS MY SEAMSTRESS CREATING MY DELICATE LACE,
MY BLOSSOM— AN UMBRELLA— A PARASOL OF GRACE.
NAMED BY A LEGEND, QUEEN ANNE WHO LOVED TO SEW,
SNIFF ME I'M A WILD CARROT, FROLICKING IN THE LUSH MEADOW.

I am Queen Anne's Lace

I'M AS CUDDLY AS CAN BE,
CHILDREN DELIGHT IN SEEING ME.
GOLDEN SUNNY POM—POM HEADS,
CHEERFUL AND BRIGHT AS A CHILD ONCE SAID.

I'm a Teddy Bear Sunflower

SOFT AND FUZZY THAT'S WHAT I AM,
VELVET AND WOOLY, JUST LIKE A LAMB.
WHISPER GENTLY INTO MY EAR,
A SILENT "BAA" YOU'RE BOUND TO HEAR.

I am a Lamb's Ear

LIKE PEAS IN A POD, MY SEEDS DO GROW,
MY VINES THEY CLIMB FROM ROW TO ROW.
MY PALETTE OF COLORS KNOWS NO END,
FRAGRANT AND DREAMY IN THE SPRING I ASCEND.

TAKE A STROLL DOWN MEMORY LANE,
THINK OF TIMES FROM PAST AGAIN.
SMILE UPON MY PETITE LITTLE FACE,
I'LL LIVE IN YOUR HEART, FOREVER WITH GRACE.

I am a Forget-Me-Not

SLEEK AND BRILLIANT WITH TINY BLACK SPOTS,
CAN YOU HEAR MY DEAFENING ROAR?
CALLING OUT FOR ALL TO HEAR,
MY STALK PROVIDES STRONG VIGOR.

I am a Tiger Lily

SMOOTH AND CREAMY, MY CUPS OF GOLD,
BUTTERY TO THE TOUCH.
GROWING FIVE PETALED NEAR THE POND,
"LITTLE FROG", WE LOVE YOU MUCH.*

*BOTH FROGS AND BUTTERCUPS INHABIT AREAS WITH
WATER SUCH AS SWAMPS, PONDS, LAKES, AND RIVERS.
IN LATE LATIN, THE GENUS NAME RANUNCULUS MEANS
"LITTLE FROG".

MY FUZZY BEARD ADORNS MY FACE,
GIVING ME A LOOK OF STYLE AND GRACE.
PINK, WHITE, ROSE— MY BLOSSOMS DO ATTRACT,
LURING ALL MY GARDEN FRIENDS TO ALWAYS COME ON BACK.

MILK OR DARK CHOCOLATE,
IT'S FOR YOU TO DECIDE WHAT'S BEST.
MY VELVET PETALS FRAGRANT AND LUSH,
I'M SWEETER THAN ALL OF THE REST.

I am Chocolate Cosmos

MY BLOSSOMS OF ORE, DOUBLOONS OF GOLD,
LAST ALL SEASON LONG— A STORY UNTOLD.
NAMED AFTER MARY, A SMALL ENGLISH GIRL,
MY BRIGHT ROUNDED PETALS, OH HOW THEY UNFURL!

I am a Marigold.

BLUE AND COMPACT, I AM A LITTLE MOUND,
WITH EARS CURLED LIKE A MOUSE.
WITH WAXY LEAVES, I LOVE THE SHADE,
SYMMETRY ALL AROUND.

I am a Mouse Ear Hosta

SNAP, SNAP, SNAP!
OH HOW MY LITTLE FACE CAN APPEAR TO BE A TRAP!
MY MANY COLORED BLOSSOMS, SO PRETTY ON THE STEM,
AND MY FIRE BREATHING BREATH IS BRIGHTER THAN A GEM!

UNFURLING IN THE MORNING,
KNOWING MY LIFE IS FLEETING.
MY TUBULAR STAR-SHAPED GLORY,
OH HOW MY BRIGHT COLORS ARE GREETING!

I am a Morning Glory

SOAKING IN THE RAYS OF SUN,
HOPING THAT MY BLOOMING SEASON WILL NEVER BE DONE.
REGAL I STAND, BOW TO ME NOW,
WHEN OTHERS SMILE UP TO ME, THEY CAN'T HELP BUT SAY, "WOW!"

I am a Sunflower

NAMED AFTER THE PIONEER WOMEN,
SHIELDING THEIR EYES FROM THE SUN.
MY BONNET PROTECTS MY DAINTY FACE,
MY SISTERS, MY BROTHERS, AND EVERYONE.
THE SPRINGTIME FIELDS ARE COVERED IN BLOSSOMS,
IN HUES OF EVERY BLUE,
A SEA OF WONDER AND DELIGHT,
A—WAITING JUST FOR YOU!

SURPRISE! MY LITTLE KNOWN NAME IS LADY'S EARDROP,
RESEMBLING AN EARRING HANGING DOWN FROM THE TOP.
ATTRACTED BY MANY, HUMMINGBIRDS ALIGHT,
MY DRESSES OF COLOR, THEY SURE DO DELIGHT!

I am a Fuschia

MY NECTAR, IT BOASTS THE SWEETEST OF TASTES,
ATTRACTING FRIENDS FROM ALL AROUND.
LOVING THE SUN, MY VINES FRAGRANT AND FUN,
AROUND THE TRELLIS I CREEP AND ABOUND.

I am a Honeysuckle

MY DELICATE BLOOMS CARRY LOVE SO DEEPLY,
MY HEART IS ON MY CHEST.
FILLED WITH EMOTION FOR EVERY DAY,
LIFE IS A BEAUTIFUL QUEST.

I am a Bleeding Heart

MY "DAY'S EYE" TRACKS THE SUN,
MY DELICATE PETALS OPEN ONE BY ONE.
AT DUSK I SLOWLY SHUT EACH EYE,
AND SLUMBER SWEETLY THROUGH THE NIGHT.

I am a Daisy

MY PRETTY LITTLE BLUE STARS CREEPING ALL AROUND,
SPREADING OUT MY TENDRILS ALL OVER THE GROUND.
WHAT EARTHLY CONSTELLATIONS DO YOU SEE UPON ME?
I MAKE A COZY LANDING SPOT FOR THE BIG BUMBLE BEE.

I am Blue Star Creeper

LIKE AN URCHIN IN A TIDE POOL,
I LIVE ON LAND, AN EXCEPTION TO THE RULE.
MY GRASSY GREEN FINGERS, WAVES OF THE SEA,
PINCUSHION BLOSSOM—HEADS BOBBLE WITHIN ME.

I am a Sea Thrift

MY SEED PODS RESEMBLE THE FOOT OF A BIRD,
MY BLOSSOMS OF YELLOW AND GOLD.
BLOOMING PROFUSELY WHEREVER I ROAM,
OTHERS MUNCH ON MY FOLIAGE UNTOLD.

I am a Bird's Foot Trefoil

MY FRIENDS FROM THE SEA, THEY DO CALL TO ME,
BUT MY PLACE ON THE LAND IS MY TRUE DESTINY.
DING DONG! MY TALL SPIKES CHIME,
IMPRESSIVE FOLIAGE COLOR THAT LASTS A LONG, LONG TIME.

I am a Coral Bell

A CARPET OF BRIGHT COLOR, MY LEAVES DO SHIMMER,
REFLECTING TINY CRYSTALS OF ICE.
OPEN, THEN SHUT, MY EYES THEY ARE A-WINKING,
I'M HAPPY IN A SUNNY PARADISE.

I am an Ice Plant

MY BUTTONS NEED NO SEWING,
ADORNED IN VIBRANT BLUE.
YOU WILL BE HARD—PRESSED TO FIND LOVE,
IN ANY BETTER HUE.

I am a Bachelor Button

MY DARK EYES A–GAZIN',
LOOKING TO THE SUN.
BLESSED BE MY LONG BLOOMING SEASON,
GOLDEN PETALED, I AM SUSAN.

STANDING TALL WITH TUBES OF SWEETNESS,
BEES SWIFTLY BUZZING BY.
MY PAINTED FRECKLES ARE QUITE THE ATTRACTION,
FOR EVERY BUTTERFLY.

I am a Foxglove

MY GARDEN OF WONDER AND COLOR AND DELIGHT,
I AM ALWAYS IN AWE AS I GAZE AT THIS SIGHT.
NATURE IS BEAUTY I JUST HAVE TO SAY
GO OUT AND SEE IT AND EXPLORE IN IT TODAY!

Author's Note

As an author, I have greatly enjoyed getting the opportunity to be able to write this book. Ever since I can remember, I have always loved flowers and gardening i my own yard, which is part of my inspiration for this book, and also why, on a personal level, this book is so special to me.

When I was picking the flowers that were going to be featured in this book, I go the fun idea of including flowers with different, clever, or unique names. I wanted to be able to make poems that really connected with each flower's name, and my goal was to almost explain each flower's name through a poem. I definitely had lots of fun thinking and researching all kinds of different fun-named flowers to put in this book!

This book is not your average children's picture book, because each poem is so specific, focusing on the little details of beauty and the attributes of each and every flower. I had to do a lot of research and studying about traits, nicknames, and interesting characteristics of each flower. I'll admit, it took me a while to finally be satisfied with my work and the rhyme schemes. I felt such a sense of "needing to get it just right" for every flower, as each is unique and beautiful in its own way; therefore, each flower poem is a stand-alone literary creation. Also, I love how the illustrator, Tatiana, had the idea to dress each flower fairy in the essence of the flower blossom featured from each poem. Those fairies are just so charming, and I appreciate Tatiana's incredibly thoughtful works of art!

Each poem in this book is kind of like a riddle. The poems are almost tempting you, the reader, to try and figure out (based on the clues you can find in the poem about each flower) what kind of flower it could possibly be! My thought was that the reader could have lots of fun guessing and trying to figure out the riddle of the flower on each page.

In addition, the bumble bee hidden on each page is definitely one of my favorite parts of this book. When I was younger I would always pour over I-Spy and Seek-and-Find books, trying to find all the hidden things and having a blast while doing it. It was one of my favorite things to do! That's part of the reason that I wanted to add a bumble bee that was hidden on each page- to not only make this a children's picture book that everybody could enjoy, but to be able to add another element of fun to my book. I also had two very special little friends in mind when I came up with this idea! My two-year-old cousin, Lily, always loves to help me "find the bumble bee" on my illustrations, and she also loves to help me "work" on my book whenever I'm editing or writing. My other little special friend who I had in my mind is a three-year-old family friend named Quinn. I know that she loves reading my previous book, <u>My Oregon</u>, and that she also enjoys fairies and flowers. So, thank you young ladies for helping me with a lens for this book! You girls are very special.

Lastly, I also decided that I will donate a portion of my book proceeds to organizations that help save our endangered bumble bees who so desperately need our help. I hope that this will inspire others to help save these creatures too. I encourage everyone to consider planting bee-loving plants as well.

I hope that you enjoy reading this book and that it will inspire you to go outside and enjoy nature, wherever you are. You can find beauty everywhere in the amazing outdoors.

Thank you for all of your support.
Brigette Harrington, Author

About The Author

Brigette Harrington resides in Hillsboro, Oregon with her parents and her two cats, Apollo and Persephone.
She is 12 years old and is in the 7th grade.
In her spare time, she loves to garden, write, read, and craft.
She also avidly plays the violin and piano. She currently has two published books, <u>My Oregon</u> and <u>If Flowers Could Talk</u>.
Be sure to check out her website at AbeoBooks.com to find out more about Brigette, her books, and new updates.

About the Illustrator

Hi there. My name is Tatiana Rusakova.
I'm a book illustrator living in the Ukraine. I really love my job. I think
I'm incredibly lucky to create books for kids in collaboration with
amazing authors from all over the world.
This book took me one year to complete, but I was very thrilled
to work on it, because plants and flowers are my passion.
Brigette and I invite you into this magic world of flowers.
We hope you will like this journey.

www.rusakova.com.ua
rusakova.art@gmail.com